In Memory of

MARAGRET M. McILVAINE

1996

THIS IS A IS A GREAT PLACE FOR A HOT DOG STAND

BARNEY SALTZBERG

Hyperion Books for Children
New York

For my father, with love and sauerkraut

Izzy hated his job. He worked in a toy factory, painting Baby Beastie horns. The smell of paint made Izzy sick.

Izzy left the factory on his
lunch hour. He would take long,
slow, deep breaths of the world
outside, where he longed to be.

One afternoon he smelled
something so delightful
that it made his mouth water.
Izzy felt as if he were floating over
a carnival on a hot summer's day.

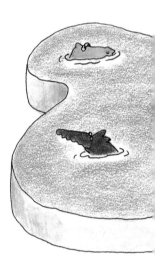

A hot dog vendor wheeled her hot dog stand right past his nose. The wonderful aroma gave Izzy an idea.

That night Izzy built his own hot dog stand.

He quit working at the factory and
set out to find a place to sell hot dogs.

Izzy pushed his stand until he came to the top of a hill with a beautiful view.

"Ahh. Fresh air!" he said.

"This is a great place for a hot dog stand!"

Izzy waited. Nobody came.
He didn't mind. He was happy being outdoors.
In the afternoon there were still no customers.
In fact, it was so quiet, Izzy fell asleep.

By the end of the day, Izzy hadn't
sold a single hot dog. Maybe this
wasn't such a good place for a
hot dog stand after all, he thought.

The next morning Izzy followed the scent of green grass and trees to a crowded park. "This is a great place for a hot dog stand!" he said.

"You're right," he heard someone say.
"My grandfather sold hot dogs here.
My father sold hot dogs here.
And now *I* do! So why don't you
follow your nose somewhere else?"

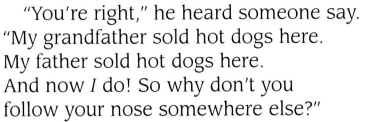

"Selling hot dogs is harder
than I thought," said Izzy.

Izzy wandered down a street and noticed a tiny dirt lot between two old buildings. He looked around. Busy neighborhood, he thought.

Izzy sniffed for a moment. "I can't smell anybody selling hot dogs. It's settled. This is a great place for a hot dog stand!"

Izzy cleared away the weeds and hauled away the trash.
When the lot was clean he parked his hot dog stand.
Izzy took out two different kinds of mustard,
a jumbo bottle of ketchup, and jars filled with all sorts
of wonderful things to pile on top of hot dogs.

Even before Izzy had a chance to chop the onions,
he sold his first hot dog.
Izzy was delighted.

Soon everyone in the neighborhood knew about Izzy's hot dogs.

And once you ate at Izzy's, he never forgot your name or how you liked your hot dog.

Gertie loved hot dogs with pineapple sauce—twice a day!

Zeppo always ordered a chutney chicken dog with a squirt of ketchup and three scoops of relish.

Izzy always remembered.

Ned ate a kielbasa dog on a sesame bun every Tuesday at a quarter past noon.
Izzy always had it ready.

Sometimes Izzy knew what type of hot dog
a new customer would like just by looking at his face.

Izzy knew he had found the perfect place to sell hot dogs.
He decided to build a permanent stand so everyone
would always know where he'd be.

When the new stand was finished it looked like a giant hot dog.
Visitors came from miles around just to take a peek.
Izzy was happy.

One afternoon a man who introduced himself as Earl stopped by for a turkey dog with extra onions.

"Nice place for a hot dog stand," said Earl.

"I know," said Izzy.

"Too bad you have to move," said Earl.

6. MAX ONIO

7. IZZY   SAUER KRAUT

8. RUTHIE   TOFU, SPICY MUSTARD

GERTIE   PINEAPPLE SAUCE

EPPO   CHICKEN DOG WITH CHUTNEY

Izzy watched Earl swallow his hot dog in one bite. Izzy could smell trouble.

"I've got orders to knock this block down," said Earl. "A Mega Mall is going up."

"But I just built this hot dog stand!" said Izzy.

Earl handed Izzy a green piece of paper. It was an official-looking letter from a Madame Moola Moo. It said she owned the block and that a Mega Mall was to be erected on that very site. If there were any questions, she could be reached at her home in Heiferville.

Earl crunched his napkin into a ball and dropped it in the trash. "I guess it wasn't such a great place for a hot dog stand!" he said before he left.

By that afternoon Izzy's customers had heard the bad news.
They paraded up and down the block carrying signs and chanting,
"Save Izzy's! Save Izzy's!"

Izzy wasn't waiting for the wrecking crew. He ran off to Heiferville, where he found Madame Moola Moo walking her dog Hoola.

Izzy introduced himself to Madame Moola Moo.

"You see," said Izzy, "I built this hot dog stand on the lot between your two buildings. It's called Izzy's. I named it after myself!"

"I'm not interested in hot dog stands," said Madame Moola Moo.

"It's more than a hot dog stand,"
said Izzy. "It's a place where it doesn't matter
if you have scales or fur;
if you're green, purple, or blue;
if you like knockwurst or kosher.
It's a place to take a few minutes of your day
to stop and enjoy one of life's
last simple, succulent wonders.
A hot dog!
   "If you would only come see
my hot dog stand, you wouldn't
want to tear it down."

"I don't have time to fly off
and see a hot dog stand!"
said Madame Moola Moo.
"I'm busy, busy, busy! I build malls!
Besides, I've got to go buy
Hoola a new sweater."

"At least have a hot dog!" said Izzy.
As Madame Moola Moo left, Izzy
handed her a tofu dog with
sauerkraut, mustard, and grilled onions.

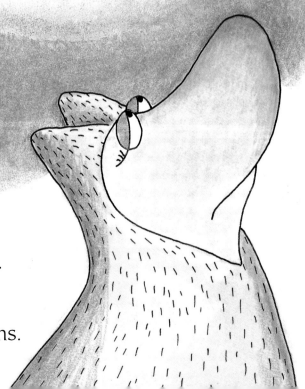

When Izzy went back the wrecking crew was setting up.

I thought Madame Moola Moo would change her mind, thought Izzy. Maybe I put too many onions on her tofu dog!

The truck with the wrecking ball pulled up in front of his hot dog stand. Izzy covered his eyes.

"Wait!" someone shouted. "What's that up in the sky?"
Izzy looked up. A helicopter hovered overhead, lowering
a figure down to the ground.

Madame Moola Moo landed in front of the hot dog stand.
"Do you have any more of those tofu dogs?" she asked.
Izzy smiled. "Would you like a drink with that?" he asked.
"Most extraordinary!" said Madame Moola Moo
as she looked at Izzy's hot dog stand.

"Please, please, please don't make Izzy move!" cried Zeppo.
"I eat a chutney chicken dog at Izzy's every day of the year.
He even puts a sparkler in my hot dog for the Fourth of July!"

"There's only one thing to do!"
said Madame Moola Moo.
She picked up one of the
Save Izzy's signs and
held it high in the air.

When the mall was finished,
Izzy's hot dog stand
stood proudly in the middle.

"You were right all along!"
said Madame Moola Moo.
"This is a great place for a hot dog stand!"

First Edition
1 3 5 7 9 10 8 6 4 2

Library of Congress Cataloging-in-Publication Data
Saltzberg, Barney
This is a great place for a hot dog stand / by Barney Saltzberg—
1st ed.
p. cm
Summary: Izzy tries to save his hot dog stand from Madame Moola
Moo, who is planning to build a shopping mall on the same spot.
ISBN 0-7868-0070-4 (trade)—ISBN 0-7868-2057-8 (lib. bdg.)
[1. Business enterprises—Fiction.] 1. Title.
PZ7.S1552Th 1994 [Fic]—dc20 94-22503 CIP AC

This book is set in 14-point ITC Leawood Book.

The artwork for each picture is prepared using acrylic paint, pen and ink,
colored pencil, and Dr. Martin's dyes.